The West Door

Also by Alfred Corn:

ALL ROADS AT ONCE

A CALL IN THE MIDST OF THE CROWD

THE VARIOUS LIGHT

NOTES FROM A CHILD OF PARADISE

THE METAMORPHOSES OF METAPHOR
(essays)

The West Door

POEMS BY

Alfred Corn

VIKING

VIKING

Published by the Penguin Group
Viking Penguin Inc., 40 West 23rd Street,
New York, New York 10010, U.S.A.
Penguin Books Ltd, 27 Wrights Lane,
London W8 5TZ, England
Penguin Books Australia Ltd, Ringwood,
Victoria, Australia
Penguin Books Canada Ltd, 2801 John Street,
Markham, Ontario, Canada L3R 1B4
Penguin Books (N.Z.) Ltd, 182–190 Wairau Road,
Auckland 10, New Zealand

Penguin Books Ltd, Registered Offices:
Harmondsworth, Middlesex, England

First published in 1988 by Viking Penguin Inc.
Published simultaneously in Canada

Grateful acknowledgment is made for permission to
translate the following copyrighted works:

"Dora Markus" from *Selected Poems* by Eugenio Montale.
Copyright © 1957 by Arnaldo Montadori Editore;
Copyright © 1965 by New Directions Publishing Corporation.

"The Poet's Obligation" from *Fully Empowered* by Pablo Neruda.
Copyright © 1967, 1969, 1970, 1975 by Alastair Reid.
Used by arrangement with Farrar, Straus and Giroux, Inc.

Pages vii–viii constitute an extension of this copyright page.

Library of Congress Cataloging in Publication Data
Corn, Alfred, 1943–
The west door.
I. Title.
PS3553.0655W47   1988   811'.54   87-40299
ISBN 0-670-81956-5

Printed in the United States of America by
Haddon Craftsmen, Scranton, Pennsylvania
Set in Bodoni Book
Designed by Beth Tondreau Design

In Memoriam David Kalstone

and for
J. McC., J.B.,
B.H., and T.R.

Acknowledgments

Poems appeared in the following publications, sometimes in different form:

The Agni Review, "Prophet Bird"
The Amicus Journal, "Duck Pair" and "Wintergreen Retablo"
BeanFeast, "The Column"
The Boston Review, "A Little Lower Than the Angels"
Columbia, "Archaic Torso of Apollo" and "The Poet's Task"
Four Quarters, " 'Nina' at the Phoenix Park Zoo" and "Stephen Dedalus: Self-Portrait as a Young Man"
Grand Street, "Two Travelers on a Summer Evening" and "Toward Skellig Michael"
Jacaranda, "Dogwood" and "Old Lang Synes"
Margin (U.K.), 'Welcome to Farewell"
The Nation, "Before They Wake"
The New Republic, "The Band" and "Assistances"
New Virginia Review, "Home Thoughts in Winter, 1778"
The New Yorker, "Naskeag" and "Wild Carrot"
Paris Review, "Apartment on 22nd Street," "Dora Markus," "Prayer to Aphrodite," and "Lost and Found"
Partisan Review, "Letter to Teresa Guiccioli"
Pequod, "Light Tasks" and "Tercina: Winter in Vermont"
Ploughshares, "Maple Canon" and "Trout and Mole"
PN Review (U.K.), "From the United Provinces" and "*Navidad*, St. Nicholas Ave."
Poetry, "The Chi-Rho Page from the Book of Kells" and "An Xmas Murder"
Shenandoah, "From the United Provinces"
The Southwest Review, "Paranoiad"
The Threepenny Review, "Dublin, the Liberties"
The Yale Review, "The Candlelight Burglary"

The sequence *Tongues on Trees* was first published as a chapbook by Parenthèse Editions.

"An Xmas Murder" was published by Sea Cliff Press.

"The Column" and "New Year" were first published by Friday Imprints.

"*Navidad*, St. Nicholas Ave." was published by Albondocani Press.

The author wishes to thank the Guggenheim Foundation and the New York Foundation for the Arts for fellowships during which some of the poems in this volume were written.

Contents

The West Door

The Band

Two, sometimes three come without being called.
Strictly breathing, down cool passageways
Where the hangings are (in silk cord,
Fable of the boar hunt) I go toward them.
Each one assumes a foregone expression.

(To have known the struggle'd turn literal
And still fathomed so deep, so free and dark?
I hadn't stopped to choose. But a cloudy voice
Spoke and reminded me that even a human
Face at point-blank range is a cyclops.)

They send me on, bathed in baptismal sweat
At the photographic daybreak—
Abdication more, it seemed, than dismissal.
My nearest chance was to be small, private,
Bold as a child. (Who, eyes lowered, keeps his counsel.)

Naskeag

Once a day the rocks, with little warning—
not much looked for even by the spruce
and fir ever at attention above—
fetch up on these tidal flats and bars.
Large, cratelike rocks, wrapped in kelp;
layer on imprinted layer,
umber to claret to olivegreen,
of scalloped marbling. . . .
Not far along the path of obstacles
and steppingstones considered,
fluid skeins of bladder wrack
lie tufted over the mussel shoals—
the seabed black as a shag's neck,
a half-acre coalfield, but alive.
Recklessly multiple, myriads compact,
the small airtight coffers (in chipped enamel)
are starred over with bonelike barnacles
that crackle and simmer throughout the trek,
gravel-crepitant underfoot.

Evening comes now not with the Evening
Star, but with a breathing fog.
And fog is the element here,
a new term, vast by indefinition,
a vagrant damping of the deep tones
of skies and bars and sea.
Sand, mud, sand, rock: one jagged pool
basining a water invisible
except as quick trembles

over algal weed—itself
half-absent, a virid gel.
Walking means to lose the way
in fog, the eye drawn out to a farther point,
a dark graph on the faint blue inlet watershine;
out to where a heron stands,
stationing its sharp silhouette
against the fogbright dusk.
Then, not to be approached,
lifts off and rows upward, *up, up,*
a flexible embracing-forward on the air,
rising out of view
behind an opaque expanse of calcium flame.

The great kelp-dripping rocks,
at random positions,
lost in thought and dematerializing
with the gray hour,
release, indelibly, their pent-up contents.
—Even the scattered feathers here
are petrified, limewhite blades and stony down.
The sky, from eastward, deepens
with the dawning insight
as the seas begin to rise, the flats
slide away, the hulls bear off the ground,
and the eye alien to so self-sufficing
a tidal system turns and takes up how to
retrace the steps that brought it there.

Two Travelers on a Summer Evening

Unbroken stillnesses: the lake mist
Set for the night, an eggshell stratum
The pines bend and brace against.
Overhead has been stretched a panel
Less or more than sky, an
Unbounded, featureless null
The grain and bark-brown of aged silk.
—Under which, a temple in tiers (two, no, three)
Deep in the background and rightfully small,
With upcurving, cat's-paw eaves,
And roofs the sort they always tile.
Crags. Low hills. Light falling. . . .
The human element here, a spindly next
To a thickset figure, almost escapes
Notice at first survey. Calligraphic, complex,
When magnified, they respond—starting with perhaps
The far one's hat, straw-golden, a conic section
He wears as shelter and emblem
(*Monk bearing staff*) of his calling.
Zeal urges him a pace beyond the factotum
(Freehand topknot, tense calves exposed)
Who makes steadily forward under a yoke—bamboo—
His arms looped up over the crossbar
With dangling bundles neatly matched
In a weight-to-weight correspondence.
Ten thousand invisible gnats.
A low frog gong from the lilypads expounds, expands. . . .
One footbridge (slatted); *two* rocks; *four* swallows.
The five, this time, fell out as barbed-wire pines

(Standing, decidedly, for long life).
Weary travelers. But can they plausibly,
This muggy twilight, be very near their goal?—
The burnished image throned inside half smiling,
Its old beatitude a certainty
That pilgrims would be drawn there to the end of time.

She looks for them again in the lower right
Of the taut silk pane (a squared circle, corners rounded)
And tilts its gleaming stem back and forward,
Paddling aside flies (come here from where?) and gnats
In warm gusts around her armchair. Hangchou:
The Southern Sung. By the West Lake, at dusk,
Heaven-blessed, willow-crowded banks stir,
Sigh, and leave little to the imagination. . . .
There, according to the poet (according to Lin-Chi),
"They forget their Southern exile,
And take Hangchou for K'ai-feng."

From the United Provinces, 1632–1677

1.
Spinoza in the Hague

Glass of the lens he ground to perfect pitch
Infused his lungs year in, year out; and took
His breath away, and slowed the patient book.
His monument, it stood to Reason, which
Was Revelation for the honest man.
Mastering Latin and Descartes, he lost
The shelter of the fathers' law—almost
His life when that mad rabble who'd killed Jan
De Witt came snarling to his door, *a Jew,*
Oh worse, an atheist. . . . In breathing calm
He waited for the preordained. And knew,
According to his mathematic psalm,
This finite world would not be merely good:
The Infinite had made it *all* He could.

2.
Vermeer of Delft

Very little can be known for certain.
His name plunged deep into his pictures, rooms
That want to tell what muted fable looms
For the voyeur who gently draws a curtain.
The Artist in His Studio, intent
On his shy model, paints her laurel crown,
Blue pinnates against the canvas. Down

Below, his stockings redden and seem to hint
At even-tempered desires. For always She
Is present, keyboard pupil, servant, wife,
Scribbler of heartfelt notes who has scattered sand
To dry her page. . . . As lilting chance has planned,
It covers everything, it glistens—this life
A stream of music and mutability.

A Little Lower Than the Angels

Eastbound jets close the day up early,
Time, like distance, paid for dearly.
My executive seatmate knows it best.
But says things could be worse. Depressed?
Not even when the market is!
Play the game for the lark it is.
Only live once, so don't drop the ball.
"Article here in *Ports of Call*—
The Astronauts. They all of them say
They'd go right back if they had their way.
Interested? Page seventy-one."
Already read it. And there goes the sun.
Isn't it time they brought our drinks?
"Pan Am Airlines' service *stinks*.
Me, haven't touched it since '66.
Scotch and my heart rate didn't mix."
Ruefulness engraves fine crinkle-lines
Around his eye, whose pupil shines.
I smile (as all his clients do?)
And see he thinks I'm OK too.
Higher, darker, our homeward flight.
My friend reaches up and turns on the night.

Lost and Found

No one but the prodigal returns.
Extravagance, the same as parsimony,
Disguised a bent for pillaging oneself?
To keep the homeward track, though, asked not dwelling
on the irrecoverable, not counting how many
moons were spent, fistfuls of coin sent rolling
on the green baize at two A.M., the jokes,
riots, banquets laid for spangled throngs
whose bellowed toasts would fan the smoky uproar.

Amusement scaled like a mountain, rapture
run through and shed like a skin,
the protocols of aftermath
gestured their subject into a valley
it took pain to unlock the meaning of—
as though along with ripped-out checks
sown left and right had fled some blunt specie
of imperception, a former deafness
to mumbled fear that clambered up now
from a foxhole, or grief betrayed
by signs tenuous as ragged breathing
in a darkened room till now ignored
though it had waited there half a life.

Home: the blessed ordeal of being
irreplaceable, forgiven, ushered down
a dim passage of hand-polished memories,
and left alone among their silent welcome.
The young master a beggar in beat-up shoes?—

Whose sister steals in with cloth and basin,
eyes widening at the dust that streaks his face.
The world collects its debts, that is its job.
But she, with the clairvoyant ease
of the long-standing ancillary, smiles
and touches on favorite instances
of childhood mutiny that saw them together
ferreting up and down the stairs, partners
in adventure, those days. . . .
                           And he will do what now?
First, for his father's sake, accept the honor
of one more feast, traditional, the milk-fed calf
solemnly slaughtered and presented—fresh substance,
new life—to all the household.
Then take up whatever tasks fall to his hand—
husbandry, repairs, accounts, improvements—
and find a path to terms with his brother's
righteous indignation, gnarled
and rooted like the olive tree.

Before They Wake

The early riser
who took his coffee outdoors
for an outside view
on his weathered frame house
leans knee-up against
the dry-stone wall
beside the garden path.
Not yet gone by, forty pink
candles, the October
asters shift and glow.
He reads, doesn't read; and will
soon fold the morning paper,
hoist up on haunches,
reach for the cool handle
of the heavy cup, noticing
small, hoarse bell strokes
when it slips and jars
on the flagstone;
so that one round
pawprint of velvet
grown fast attached
makes a brief green signal
as he glances down, crouched
over the gray slate
shot through with silver wires.
Then the milkglass air
will drain a step
lighter up the scale,
an entire staggering flight,

and blood pound black tympani
in the inner ear:
the fadeout colors,
stream of all that is
passing together with all
the tender, unquenchable—.
Damn. Stood up too fast.
But the strewn leaves focus,
the sprawling stalks
steady themselves; the sun
dims to bright again.
Open, dark, the screened
door's a dozen loping paces away.
Back in now, just to see?
Spurred to no rigid purpose
but astride feeling
this age exactly;
and also with company
(hear them inside)
stirring, about to come down.

Tercina: Winter in Vermont

They say a freezing water-table
Brings down the Fahrenheit of desire.
And yet the stream's human laughter

Was something more than a baleful after-
Word. Indirection, slow but able,
Leaves almost nothing to desire?

Yes! though that ice skate named Desire
Glide to the tune of gales of laughter.
Given so much that's lamentable. . . .

Desire "expects some laughter at table."

The Candlelight Burglary

Open the vacation house after a winter's absence
And always some surface or hidden damage lies in wait—
Which goes to confirm the adage, still not obsolete,
That nothing really ever lasts but Time itself.
This year, it took the form of a second-story man;
Amateur, a detective also amateur would judge
From simple clues: a punched-in glass pane and (power
Was off) quick recourse to a candle-end, abandoned
On the mantel first by host and then by visitor—
This marble-pale wand, guttered, with a black wire
At its core. Wouldn't anyone have thought to bring
A flashlight? Well, a stand-in was near and apropos,
Provided by the absentee. "Through all her kingdoms,
Nature insures herself." True, and someone has to make
An inventory: *landscape with boy angling in rushing
Stream; music system, more or less new; a chiming clock;
A Federal mirror. . . .* Portable, negotiable,
They were what attracted his quick sleights of hand.
(At least the silver knew enough to stay in hiding.)
I'm sure this place was only one of several targets;
And then, effects not used nine months a year, we can
Obviously live without, hence may not have a right to. . . .

But look, now the hindered title, at one stroke,
Breaks free: mine—the law says so—if stolen from me.
(As losses help the gambler own up to what he lacks?)
In each drawer jerked open, a starry splash of marble,
Tears spilled over things taken, or rather those
Left behind for me to try to have and hold. . . . Imagine

The scene in eerie chiaroscuro that sprang into life
For that carpenter ant typing his way across the sill,
Who, how many nights ago, paused, antennae extended
At a blocklike grain of sugar, saw its quartz sparkle
In the glow and waver of invasive light, and then
A distant, crouching prowler, almost giant as his shadow.
A witness so marginal could hardly identify
Or think valuable what was spirited away
On the spread wings of cupidity-with-mind-made-up. . . .
Nor have followed the implications of a psyche's forcing
The issue, fear of discovery, of loss, the curious
Unconsidered spilling of light (and burning wax)
On all that's truly worth having. Worth having, that is,
When we keep, among other uninsurables, our word—
Goods possessed, for the most part, courtesy of darkness,
Which keeps things secret and doing so keeps them.

An Xmas Murder

He sits at the table, cloudlight of March
One tone with his hair, gray-silver on silver.
Midday fare in Vermont is basic enough.
In West Newbury, eggs and toast will do—
Though our doctor's had his sips of wine as well.
"Just don't be fooled. They're not as nice as you
Think they are. Live here a few more winters,
You'll get to know them clearer, and vice-versa."
Three years now, and we're still finding our way;
Newcomers need a guide to show them the ropes,
And he has been explaining township and county
Almost from the sunstruck day we met him
That very first July in this old house.
"I'll cite an instance of community
Spirit at work, North Country justice—
A case I just happened to be involved in.
No, please—all right, if you are having one."
He holds his glass aloft and then lets fall
A silence that has grown familiar to us
From other stories told on other days,
The will to recount building its head of steam.
"Well, now, you have to know about the victim.
His name was Charlie Deudon, no doubt Canuck
Stock some generations back, but he
Nor no one else could tell you—if they cared.
Deudons had been dirt farmers here as long
As anybody knew. They never starved
But never had a dime to spare, either.
Charlie resolved to change the Deudon luck.

And that's just what he did. Or almost did. . . .
He'd graduated two classes ahead of mine;
We knew each other, naturally, but not
On terms of friendship. Fact is, he had no friends,
And only one girlfriend, whom he married
Day after Commencement, June of '32.
And then he set to work and never stopped
Again, until they made him stop for good."
A wisp of a smile, half irony, half
Bereavement plays about his guileless face—
Red cheeks, blue eyes, a beardless Santa Claus;
Whose bag contains (apart from instruments
Of healing) stories, parables and proverbs,
Painkillers, too, for when all else fails.
"What kind of work had all that hard work been?"
"Oh, farming, like his elders, only better.
All the modern improvements, fancy feed
And fertilizers, plus machinery—
He was the first in these parts to milk
His herd in any way but as 'twas done
Since Adam's boys first broke ground with a plow.
And anything machines couldn't handle,
Charlie did himself, from dawn to midnight.
He never wasted a word or spilled a drop
Of milk or drank a drop of beer or liquor.
He was unnatural. *And* he made that farm
Into a showplace, a kind of 4-H model.
He made good money, yes, but not a dollar
Would he spend unnecessarily.

Do you get the picture? They hated him,
The boys that hung around the package store.
The most they ever got from tightfist Charlie
Deudon was a nod out from under his cap.
(His trademark—a baseball cap striped white and red.)
They envied him for getting his hay in first;
And there was more. A boy that he had hired,
By the name of Carroll Giddens, was their buddy.
Likeable fellow, regulation issue,
The sort that knocks back a pint or a fifth
In half a shake and tells off-color stories
Till he's got them choked to death with laughing.
'Course the wisecracks they loved best were those
About poor Charlie and his gold-plated farm. . . .
Just one more case of what's been often said
By commentators on democracy—
How it helps everyone keep modest."
Teasing mischief has crept into his voice.
A self-taught anthropologist as well
As teller of tales, he has other frames
Of reference to place around events
Local or international. He knows
That things can stand for more than what they are;
Indeed, says standing for things is why we're here,
And quotes chapter and verse to prove his point.
"Think of the worldwide scapegoat ritual.
In halfway civilized societies
An animal's the one relieved from life
Duty, am I right? A fellow tribesman

Will do in a pinch, if animals are lacking,
Or if communal fears get screwed too tight. . . .
Anyhow, it was clear that something more
Than common envy stirred up the lynch law.
Their own failure's what they wanted dead."
Seconds pass in silence as he stares
At something—perhaps a knothole in the pine
Floorboard. He looks up, eyebrows raised,
And twirls the glass stem between stubby fingers.
A coil of rope hung on the wall, we see,
Has made him pause and heave reflective sighs.
"Here. Have another. So: was Charlie punished?"
"I'm going to tell you—better me than others.
You see, I was involved—no, no, no,
Not in the deed, Lord, no, just as a witness.
It happened this way—hope you're not squeamish.
Charlie had this boy to help with chores,
The one named Carroll. Married, two kids, I think.
Not too reliable. But so few are;
Nor could you call his wages generous.
His buddies must have stood him drinks, is all
I can say. He'd a skinful half the time—
Was certainly drunk that Christmas Eve morning.
No reason to doubt what Charlie told his wife.
Charlie'd been up to help at six with the milking,
And Carroll, drunk as a fiddler's bitch, was there
Loading a pair of milk cans into the barrow.
He took a slip and the whole business spilled.
Wooden handle clipped him in the side,

And he fell, too, right in the puddle of milk.
And started *laughing*. Charlie, you can guess,
Didn't join in; he told him to get on home.
'What about the milk?' 'Go home,' he said,
'You're drunk.' 'But what about the milk?' asks Carroll.
'Comes out of next week's paycheck,' Charlie says.
And then the trouble starts, with Carroll swearing
And yelping, till Charlie gives him a little tap
And goes indoors. By then Carroll could tell
The barrow handle had cracked a rib or two.
He drove into town to see his doctor—that
Wasn't me—and word went out that Charlie
Had roughed up his innocent assistant.
That's all they needed, Carroll's friends. *About
Time that stuck-up bastard got his due,
He's gone too far this time, but we'll show him,*
Et cetera. . . . As it was Christmas Eve,
They had the leisure, the liquor, and the rope."
"They hanged him?" "No, that's not our way up here.
The honored custom's to dump them in the river.
You see, the river's New Hampshire all the way
Over to the Vermont side, and thus,
If the victim's still alive when he hits the water,
New Hampshire law enforcement and legal justice
Steps in. It tends to confuse the issue, see?
In wintertime, the river freezes over,
And you can't hope to fish the bodies out
Till the month of March at the earliest.
By then, who knows which state the victim died in?

A trick they've played a hundred years and more
Up in Woodsville, where the bridge is. That's where
The loggers used to go to spend their money
On booze and hookers—who'd arrange for them
To get knocked in the head at the right moment,
And pitched off the bridge into the water.
A famous local industry, but rather
Fallen on hard days by the early fifties,
Just like others more legitimate. . . .
Well, our local rowdies knew the routine,
And, when time came to follow up their threats,
They laid their plans according to tradition.
They knew that Charlie'd have to do the milking
Christmas morning same as every day.
And when he came into the barn to do it,
They'd be waiting for him. And that's what happened."

We strain forward to hear him tell the rest;
The narrative spell is on him, and on us.
His voice weaves through fine-tuned nuances,
With sudden leaps in volume and skittish phrases
That somehow help flesh out what he describes.
We see the sprawling barn across the highway
From the white-columned porch of the old house.
See the barn closed up tight against the cold,
And the blue-gray light of December dawn
As Charlie crosses the road to do his chores.
The roosters shriek their morning alarm, the big
Doors creak open on the darkness—a darkness

Slit with tight-strung wires of light knifing
Through cracks between the boards of the east wall.
Tufts of hay spill from cribs on both sides.
The waiting cattle stir and low as daylight
Breaks in on the darkness. Their master strides
In past the parked pickup truck, his pail,
A battered Rath Blackhawk lard can swinging
At his side, a whistled "Jingle Bells"
His fight song for the working holiday.
He hears the verses harnessed to his whistling,
The tune drawing its text along march tempo:
. . . *it is to ride in a one-horse open sleigh-ay!*
And then all changes. Smash of the blackjack
Against his skull, exploding carnival
Of fire-veined shock that flies to the far corners
Of night. Four assailants leap from the back
Of the truck and lift him partly erect, the quicker
To bind his arms behind and truss them to
His half-bent legs, as you might rope a steer
Or sheep you meant to brand or slaughter.
They take him out to where the car is waiting
And throw him in the trunk like a sack of feed.
Another car drives past but doesn't slow.
The bandits duck and climb inside their own.
Tires screech, the driver slams onto the highway,
A smile and wink all round as they drive north
To Woodsville. The sun is coming up when they
Reach the bridge and stop the car. The lid
Of the trunk's sprung open, its cargo discharged.

He is dragged to the railing, lifted, then heaved over.
The body falls, seeming almost to pause
In air before it hits the water and slides
Below the surface of the floating ice. . . .
Five miles back along the highway, the dark
Barn, the herd, a crushed tin pail, and signs
Of struggle in the dirt wait for someone's
Startled face, back-lit in the doorway,
To see them, then whip aside with a shout of terror.

"He wasn't found until spring thaw; he washed
Ashore just south of Bradford, still tied up
And looking like they'd tarred and feathered him—
Partly decomposed, but not his clothes.
First thing was an autopsy to test if he
Had died by drowning or was dead before
Going under. Conclusion was, he'd died
On land, so as I said, his death belonged
To the Green Mountain State's criminal justice."
"And what about the killers—were they caught?"
"Several suspects found themselves in jail—
And that's where I come in: as star witness.
It happened I was on the road that morning.
Real early. See . . . I'd promised my house guest
Of the night—young Marine on leave—I'd drive
Him back to Lebanon to grab his bus.
I always keep my word, especially
When given in the night hours. Nice boy—
He's been a good friend ever since. We'd said

Good-bye until the next three-day pass.
Well, I was driving home like Merry Christmas.
Into the headlights comes the Deudon farm:
And then I noticed the car. A two-toned Kaiser,
Side of the road, beneath a maple tree.
Didn't know whose it was or why it was there.
I saw one face, Calvin Renfrew's, that's all.
He didn't *have* wheels so far as I knew.
Occurred to me right then that something might
Be fishy; but locals never meddle till—
Till it's too late, sometimes. I should have stopped.
They might have banged me on the head, but then—.
Well, even as it is they got revenge.
I'm still alive, however, and mean to stay so."
He laughs a low laugh that would chill the devil . . .
Then takes up the thread—how when he heard the news
About Charlie's disappearance, he drove down
To tell the state trooper what he'd seen.
"That was the very next day after Christmas.
By nightfall Calvin Renfrew and Norbert Joiner,
The owner of the car (the Kaiser), and two
Associates were in custody. But not
For long. Someone bailed them out, someone
Rich, it had to be, an enemy
Or rival of Charlie's. That's often our way,
You know, to let others fix the person
We secretly hate, then give them secret help
When they get their paws burned in the process.
A lot of people coveted that farm,

However much disparaged it was in public.
When Charlie's widow put it up for auction,
Don't imagine nobody came to bid.
I still see things of his on others' farms.
What didn't surprise me either's how the town,
Lord help me, the whole county took the side
Of those arrested against the murdered man.
They said old Charlie had it coming to him,
Treating his employee that way. Meanwhile,
Carroll had quietly slipped across the border
To Canada; no way to prove that he'd
Hardly been hurt at all. So rumor flew.
If words could put you under ground, why Carroll
Was dead and buried six times over, a martyr
Hounded to his grave by a maniac
Who should have been taken care of years ago.
These are churchgoing people, too, but they
Figure they have a special insight as
To what the Boy Upstairs considers right.
Man is born for sorrow, so we're told,
And some try to make sure he gets a close
Acquaintance with the sorrow that's his due.
Meanwhile, if you can say the things people
Want to hear, then you may lynch at will."
He folds his hands and brings them to his chin.
"The rest of the story you can figure out
Yourself. Their lawyer asked the jury be
Directed by the judge to return a verdict
Of Not Guilty. Motion granted—as never

Before for a capital offense in *this* state.
They'd do it again, don't worry, if the case
Was dear to their concerns. Sounds cynical,
I grant you. . . . But then, you see, they started next
On me for fingering the guilty parties.
State trooper drops by to ask some questions.
Why was I on the highway that time of morning?
Oh? And who exactly was this friend?
Oh, really? Stayed the night, did he? I see. . . .
A doubt or two'd been raised before already,
Given that I had never married, *and*
Was locally famous for my special hobby.
I'm sure I've told you: I play a little pipe
Organ at church sometimes—I even travel
To play it elsewhere. I know organists
All over New England, and the town gazette
Used always to mention when I went to play
At musicales in other towns and states.
Nobody thought it mattered much beforehand,
But once the tale about the serviceman
Got out, my friends, well, you can just imagine.
Overnight young Dr. Stephens was
As 'musical' as you can be and not
Get tarred and feathered. My patients, some of them,
Began to melt away like ice cream. Stephens,
A local name, respected in these parts,
Became a byword for things we don't discuss.
I wondered whether I should move, of course;
Some rowdy threw a can of paint at the house;

I still get unsigned letters from time to time.
Things must be better where you two come from.
But this is where I've always lived, it's what
I know. If I had had the sense to pitch
Someone unpopular from off a bridge
Instead of enjoying music, chances are
I'd be a favorite son. In point of fact,
I've given up the organ, seldom play it
Nowadays. I've got a different hobby—
Your health, gentlemen! No more today, though.
Another call to make this afternoon.
But listen, now: if you'll come up to me
Next week, I'll play some pump organ for you.
I can still do a rousing 'Hornpipe'—the one
By Handel. Tourist attraction hereabouts.
I am fairly confident you won't
Ever have heard it played my way before."
He stands to go, consenting to be ushered
Out under the black trees of late March, down
To where his battered station wagon sits.
Thunder of engines takes him off. . . . But his words
Stay lodged in us like arrows, arrows aimed
As carefully as acupuncture and meant
Somehow to warn or counsel. Not that warnings
In the abstract often help stave off
Particular misfortunes, inevitably
The body of most stories drawn from life.
Misfortunes are the hinges life turns on?
Reprieves as well—along with persons, places,

Passions. A fluent paradox, the realm
Normally termed external, I mean its way
Of overhearing thought and mustering
Fresh evidence. . . . Today, for instance, how
New green on branches and a liquid birdcall
Suffice to announce the chaste approach of spring.

Tongues on Trees

for John Bernard Myers

DOGWOOD

The forsythia (early because eager)
once played out, comes a second, larger
flowering to this dwarfish bentwood tree:
so christened by whoever read its emblem
for the first passion, Alpha and Omega—
one legend (deathwatch
as well) that made history?
"The flowers figure the crucifixion
with crown of stamens at the center."
Even unnoticing eyes should catch
a stigmatic, ashen, nail-
sized hole at each parchment or
rose incarnat extremity.
And at a remove (but now they) see
how the dogwood performs or prays
on itself a stunt of constriction
so as not again to grow up timber
for beams on a deicidal scale;
but bears its chiastic sprays,
blossoming X's (not bitter,
not sweet) as a kiss of peace on the wind
that says the season opens with a wound.

LIGHT TASKS

Is it penitence with head bowed,
Ecco, under the arbor roofed with wisteria,
A thousand grape stalactites, stalactites
That tune the air to a mimeo purple,
Her face filmed in monochrome as she turns
This way, closer, larger; and someone's household
China bowl of green peas brought to shell
(Each cobbled pod so many beads to tell)
For now laid aside as the wiser sister
Rises—hands extended, pale blue smile—
You all of a piece with the unforeseen?

TROUT AND MOLE

1.

Salmo gairdnerii, mercurially quick
in a thin silverfoil fish-oilskin slicker,
rash of rainbow raked along the sides,
on a whiplash tack perpetually,
tunneling through a headstream waterwall;
then sinking down to dredge among the drowsing
instars, silt, threaded algae, green-gelled light;
or planing up past clumps and globes of bubbles,
a hovel stuccoed in pearls, absences
come down piecemeal from the Above. . . .
Now something tugs upward toward the flexible, sunfired
ceiling, Something; and so with a will, higher,
a lunge up through warbled mirrorgold
into searing vacuum, brightness invisible,
arcing up to the top of his bent—and snap go
the silver shutters as the wingborne prey
(for once no useless clot of thistledown,
but a crispy bite) ephemerid! is taken.

2.

. . . down to being a starnose mole, slowly
paddling through its soupy humus (pupa, tuber,

nightcrawler eaten clean through, netted roots,
bones and pebbles clawed aside in the long
swimlike starfirst musing forward,
a darkling process moved through heavy dark);
and in his sighing night deaf to the plight
of graminifers overhead, the dandelion clocks—
O blithe geodesic feather-domes, tropisms, cortex
after electric cortex, feeling the black gnawing
underground and launching forth silk-thread asterids,
light-spirit gliders, one by one, hope against static
hope, the ten-thousand sixteenth notes of Bach's
partitas floated single file along the air, fertile,
always farther, their Garden Psalm, outward into the new. . . .

WILD CARROT

More at home than most, this immigrant
    volunteers a white roadside
hedge—and what handmade lace approaches
    the sparing extravagance
of those kaleidoscopic forms etched
    as on crystal? You'll see them,
snowcapped halves of globe (concave, sometimes,
    like Chinese bowls) and flat disks
damasked solid, or, like buttermilk
    sky, dispersed. . . . Yet all are marked
with blood-dark florets at center ruff,
    King Charles's memento mori.

It has features in common
with most parsleys (Umbelliferae),
    their intricate, fernlike leaves
and branching taproots ringed like earthworms,
    which, snapped off, smell pungent-sweet.
What's rarity, a matter of few
    numbers? Or strange perfection?
At last, exhausted with the dog days,
    the flowers close up into
tight "birds' nests," bowing to the seasons,
    to earth—where perfection goes
when there is nothing more to perfect.

DUCK PAIR

Silver water not the standard
late October chill
(and they unmindful,
lost in thought) brings first
our Doctor Mallard dressed in black
and umber, white collar, green silk cap;
his co-stroller of the river
overalled in novitiate brown
cassock, attentive, lending
her invisible ear
to Aquinas being rehearsed,
and why *aqua qua aqua* calls
for measured splashings in the element,
waterwheeling in silver unison,
wherever flowing discourse takes them,
a direct, from down, chin-tucked-under gaze
no small part of their safe-conduct—habits
by now a fact like plumage, axiomatic.

MAPLE CANON

Lordliest maple of the thick-poured trunk,
late, later, latest, still to be
treasuring so uncountably many leaves—
themselves forgetting themselves in a last
firebrand fling earthward, down
the leaning helix of a standing breeze;
to lie among the eagerer fledglings,
earlier dead, daffodil to crimson webfeet
imprinted on the icehard mud.
Each single leaf goes for a song, "sung down
by Boreas," not without thought
(in the great connective dome of νοῦς
for the never-duplicable colors
of each: there, everything that is is
recalled. Lordliest maple. . . .

WINTERGREEN RETABLO

Least ever evergreen,
forethoughtless wintergreen,
see here! a snowlit plein-air Xmas.
Then who let rain from the red candle
droplets of berries fire-engine red
—scentless as snow, oh, unlike
the leaves that crushed breathe
a green *(gloria deo)*,
degree-zero Celsius,
apple-fresh, mint-angelica flame?

OLD LANG SYNES

Medallions in several magnitudes:
  The winter midnight   solitary
For taking starviews long as these:
  And mind the diamond mallet
To strike a constellation:
  The seven-noted Pleiades
Likewise Ursa Major   Lyra and all
  Join forces in the Song remembered
Or invented of How Many Pence:
  The Song of Digging to China
Whose words are *Ewig   ewig*
  Emptiness that fills up the dark house:
Sung texts on the Not-soul
  The evertunneling void voiced
Up to the brim with whole silences:
  When thought will moult between two adamants:
Starlight: midnight: mindnight: instarlight:

Prophet Bird

They found the earth mute and passionless and left.
—Frank O'Hara

Your legend is still green with us, and avid
To demonstrate how you once scaled a mountain
Of orange crates and "knocked them down," how simply
Lifting and lighting became the Promethean blaze. . . .
Now files of ants descend on their current
Windfall, gaining focus and perhaps a better grasp
Of the unlikely but all-too-portable whole,
Which you discarded in favor of newer stages,
Reluctant to lock up a text next to its migrant
Double, the planetary warning, color of dried blood—
That impasse, too, was more than beginning
To dim and accept a kinder remnant of
Intention: the leaves turn when they fall.
We have our wishes for you still, the few
That find a rough-hewn, vine-covered lodging
For their chattels under the foothills near
Healing, variably heated springs. The ayes
And your hardly won singlings-out of praise
Befriend you for now, knowing you, enkindled
Early starling, first befriended them.

Apartment on 22nd St.

for Darragh Park

Because dusk comes in not long
after five o'clock in Chelsea
and lamps wake to life, a gold
wash falling from them,
resting on the blue-and-white,
lighting small gold clouds
in the dark wood,
or pooling in circles on the carpet;
and presumable cars whisper by
as curling leaves rattle at
the windowsill and the late hour
settles in deeper, in tune,
it could be said, with Delius on FM;
and facts, severe but familiar,
adhere to velvet, to polish, glass
and silver, and to pictures of things.
Or because calm, the readable
representation of calm, is
an achieved thing, like the last
fine overlay of glaze or light;
and because, finally, one is
entitled to a signature, affixed
now much like a reliable fact,
briskly drawn, streamlined like the city—
the painter nods and lays down his brush.

Assistances

Paris, London, Los Angeles—

men seated restlessly in a room
wait for clipped announcement of a name
grown faint and unfamiliar
to summon them upstairs.

The glare falling like cold enamel
on corked vials of venous blood,
each dyed with a message marked in code;
the dossiers that fatten
week by week, to whispered confidences
from white-clad figures in calm stances
conferring beyond the gauze of a curtain.

I think of you, friend and standard
bearer, first again to set out.
What can you not tell us about
the strong deliverance, the staggered
retreat of sound and sight,
loosing of the cord that bound
you to flesh, whose collapse still kept
a last function, the registry of pain?
Where yours ended, others take up
the relay, its sear and tremble at one
with hands that clasped, with hearts that leapt. . . .
silent injunctions made to those who wait,
balancing between patience and complaint,
until you softly call their name.

Welcome to Farewell

(Alaska)

At parallels high as these, invisible
circles, steadily more restrained,
catch last towns as they thin out
toward the Arctic vanishing point.

O perspective, give us scale
and depth, the touch to make a home
of temporary lodgings—doors opening
on new faces, the friendly lonely,
young and old,
whose year-round gazing straight up
at Polaris imparts a blue spin to their eyes;
whose voices, corrugated with magnetic North,
bark a discomposed welcome and gather us in.

Paranoiad

1.

No one listens
As magnetically. Those rife
Interpretations set you free
From doubt and error,
And the business end of your imagination
Can befriend the dread that teems in sundry—
Forms you break and recompose
Like tangrams. When you wake, how many facts
Arise, eager for you to telephone
And brief them on the new
Projections for the week,
Auspicious dates. . . . Not everything,
Of course, cooperates. Outside,
One dense, divinatory tree
Has tried to block, a bit transparently,
Interception of its leaves—
And failed. (You know its names
And habitats; detailed reports
Are being drafted even now, pivotal
For the Project "Golden Bow.")

2.

Does evidence ever lack? And what you see, others

Come to see—supplying supererogatory
Clues at your unspoken behest, the tang of meaning

As contagious and arbitrary as health itself.
Spontaneity prepense on the late-night talk show;
Repertory of team numbers assigned defensive

Linebackers in the professional leagues; sly layout
Montage of news tabloids and magazines; the casual
But fated encounter with a namesake stevedore,
Vicariously burdened, it was madness to doubt,

With your own griefs, an impromptu martyrology
Of everyday life. Brave profusion! And so many
Transmitters, there would seem almost an embarrassment
Of truth, inevitable as dawn over the world.
Yet few respond, unexhorted, to the sharp demands

Of epic existence—marathons; argosies; new
Invasions of chaos to be countered with reserve,
Loyalty, wise, premonitory orchestrations
Of will, and the almost churlish assumption of high
Destiny. . . . Yet, for the sake of argument, suppose
That someone, that *I*, had inquired about enrollment

In this discipline: the inducements that you touched on,
Would they begin with words like, "As the kaleidoscope
Encrusts with gems its snowflake rondeaux by a thousand
Hairsbreadth juxtapositions, so you will decipher
The labyrinth, thread by thread piece out its web, labor
Requiring an alertness as of the textual
Exegete minutely seizing on themes and patterns,

Yes, all the inherent detective flair long ago
Discernible in you. A rigorous calling, ours,
But so is purgation—nor can anything rival
The savage rush of insight that follows a meeting
With and vanquishing the sphinx of blank information;
Insight that once accomplished cries to the listening
Hills and valleys, 'This intends me! My story is here!'
Then perhaps a skull in the dust at your feet will seem

To whisper through its rictus and hint that neither you
Nor I have final say, are the smallest instruments
Of purposes our lot is not to fathom until
The fullness of time—if time should ever fill. Please know
That even as you plot your choices, as you dictate
Your private testament, you embody a mystery
Outside, above, and yet deep within you. Who are you
Writing? For what ear is this message? For whoever
Brought you forth into abounding strength—you, but also

Me; for the invisible author of our being
Is one whose inscrutable will and plan have involved
You in my pursuits and concern, have led me to see
You as sharing in my dreams. My secret companion,
My stowaway, the world lies before us, we have but
To go up to the place intended and name it home.'"?
But wait. Grandstanding's too easy. With designs on your
Listeners so naked, how could I or anyone
Be taken in? An orator of real cunning would
Try for a more natural, a more plausible tone.

One of us is being rather naive, aren't we?
Though clearly *you* subscribe to your every word. Don't count
On being spared as a harmless holy fool. Well, no,
I take that back. After all, you are the opposite
Sex and so qualify for special handling—not that
There have been, till now, alibis or pleas. You might say
Our relationship is like a marriage of ten years,
The first blush of romance replaced by bracing routine,
A sense of resigned disillusion, misdeeds balanced
By forbearance, weapons we would prefer not to use.
So the unwritten drama in progress is, One hand

Washes the other and *watches* the other, waiting
(Calm suspense of the DMZ) for the telltale word,
Trust itself as straw before the risk of making signs.
You say this will conclude badly. . . . There I go again,
Putting words in your mouth—where they won't melt? Nor be safe
From thieves that break in and steal. To come an unbidden
Guest under that roof would be to drown out the host—O
Eclipse! you strike the indelible gong of midnight,
So like that other universal clap of doom I
Would rather hear you speak your worst, your most abysmal
Or sardonic, anything not to contend with that
Silence which, once heard, will never hold its peace again.

Dora Markus

1.

It was where the wooden bridge
crosses to Porto Corsini on the open sea
and a few men, in slow motion, lower
or haul in their nets. With a wave
of your hand you gestured toward the other
invisible shore, your true homeland.
Then we followed the canal as far as the wharves
of the town, glistening with soot,
in that lowland where a cold spring
slowly settled down, outside memory.

And here, where a classical age
begins to break up under delicate
Asiatic tensions,
your words shimmered like rainbows on the scales
of a trout drowning in air.

Your restlessness calls to mind
birds of passage that crash against lighthouses
on stormy nights—
but your tenderness, too, is a storm,
always lowering, never breaking;
and its lulls are rarer still.
Pushed so far, how do you stay
afloat in that lake
of indifference, your heart? Perhaps
an amulet protects you, one you keep

next to your lipstick, your nail file,
your compact: a white mouse,
in ivory. *Somehow you survive!*

2.

Now, in your Carinthia,
with its flowering myrtles and little ponds,
leaning over the edge you look down
at the timid carp that gapes and swallows;
or stroll under the lindens, their crowns
thrusting up into sunset
bonfires, the waters ablaze
with awnings of landings and hotels.

The evening that stretches out
over a misty inlet brings,
above the stutter of motors,
only the cries of geese; and an interior
of snowy tiles tells
the blackened mirror that hardly
recognized you a story of errors
calmly acknowledged, engraving it within
where the dustcloth doesn't reach.

Your golden legend, Dora—
but it is already written in the fixed stares
of those men with fluffy sidewhiskers,

dignified and weak, portraits
in big gilt frames; a refrain
that comes back with every chord wrung
from the cracked barrel-organ at the hour
when dusk falls, always later and later.

It is written there. The evergreen
bayleaf all through the kitchen
survives, the voice does not fail,
Ravenna is far away; and a barbarous
creed keeps secreting its poison.
What can it want from you? None surrenders,
voice, legend, nor destiny. . . .
But it is late, always later and later.

Eugenio Montale: "Dora Markus"

Archaic Torso of Apollo

We'd had no knowledge of a head like his,
Eyes as round as fully ripened apples.
The smooth torso shines forth like a lamp
Set with his sight, which glances in steady flame

From a trimmed-down wick. Otherwise the swell
Of the chest wouldn't blind you nor a smile
Follow after the light curves of the loins
That testified in flesh to new creation.

Otherwise this stone would stand distorted,
Squat under the shoulders' translucent cascade;
It wouldn't shimmer like pelts of predators,
Wouldn't break from its confines like a star,
Brightening till the statue sees every part
Of you. You must begin a different life.

Rainer Maria Rilke: "Archaïscher Torso Apollos"

The Poet's Task

Whoever isn't listening to the sea this Friday
morning, whoever is trapped inside some
house, office, factory—or mistress
or street corner or coal mine or solitary confinement:
to that person I make my way and without speaking or nodding
come up and spring open the cage;
and something begins to hum, faint but insistent;
a great snapped-off clap of thunder harnesses itself
to the weight of the planet and the foam;
the hoarse rivers of the ocean rise up,
a star shimmers and trills in its rose window,
and the sea stumbles, falls, and continues on its way.

Then, with destiny as my pilot,
I will listen and listen harder to keep alive
in my memory the sea's outcry.
I must feel the impact of solid water
and save it in a cup outside of time
so that wherever anyone may be imprisoned,
wherever anyone is made to suffer in the dying year,
I will be there, whispering in the ceaseless tides.
I will drift through open windows,
and, hearing me, eyes will glance upward
saying, How can we get to the ocean?
And, without answering, I will pass on
the collapse of foam and liquid sand,
the salty kiss of withdrawal,
the gray keening of birds on the shore.

And so, through me, freedom and the sea
will bring solace to the downcast heart.

Pablo Neruda: "Deber del poeta"

Prayer to Aphrodite

Eternal Aphrodite, Zeus's daughter, throne
of inlay, deviser of nets, I entreat you:
do not let a yoke of grief and anguish weigh
down my soul, Lady,

but come to me now, as you did before
when, hearing my cries even at that distance
you slammed the door of your father's house—
golden! and hastened

to harness your chariot. Then pretty sparrows
drew you forthwith over the dark lands,
beating their crisp wings. From the outer spheres,
down through the inner,

steeply they descended. At last you, Divine Lady,
beaming your unearthly smile at me,
asked was I in distress once again—for,
why had I called you?

And what did my unruly heart demand
of you now? "And whom do I urge this time
to return your generous friendship? Who,
Sappho, 's been stubborn?

For if she avoids you, soon she will come
knocking; if refuses presents, will shower them
on you; if she loves not, she shall love, and
learn to be kinder."

I beg you, come. Free me from this oppression.
All that my heart longs to see accomplished,
Goddess, do it. No one could resist if you were
fighting beside me.

Sappho

Home Thoughts in Winter, 1778

(An ancestor, John Peter Corn, Virginian, native of Albemarle County, served under General Washington, in fact, was one of the ragged band that survived winter at Valley Forge. Earlier, he had been sent out with the quartermaster corps to requisition supplies for the Continental Army. Stopping at the house of a Mr. Parr in Henry County, the young soldier was led out by this landowner's daughter Hannah Elizabeth into an apple orchard. The two gathered a good supply of apples. After the truce John Peter came back to the Parrs and married Hannah Elizabeth.)

Soldier with no rank
Thus am I here
In freezing rains, in snow
And rote inactivity?
Cold, cold, this balked hunger
Blended with woodsmoke,
Clinched in creaking
Leather, coined with the ring
Of bridle and harness;
A lifted fetlock
Poises undecided
Then downclops in slush.
Numbed to speechlessness,
Infantrymen articled
To glory mere duty
Mars, waiting half
A war out, musket to shoulder—
O let it say its piece!

Speak and be silent thereafter.
In the end they *shall* bow,
And nothing then contravene us.
Home to Albemarle on foot,
An easy swing through new wheat
And orchards in flower.
At last, abject, a beggar,
Go plead for her hand.
Dark heaven, does she look
On you now, think of me still?
One goldenrod hour
Among old trees and windfalls,
She reached, turned, and said,
Quietly, "I am Hannah.
Our hopes go with the soldiers.
Here: these are red and sweet.
Others, too, we may gather,
As many as you will."

Letter to Teresa Guiccioli

Pietro's letter will have satisfied you
With the account of our health and safety.
We are tolerably tranquil—and except
An earthquake or two daily—(one of which
Broke the Lambico for filtering the water)
They rock us to and fro a little—things
Are much as when we wrote before. I miss
Last year's travels, the stops at Ithaca
And other places to which the remembrance of
Ulysses and his family are attached.
Of political news we can say but little
As little is actually known—and even that
Partly contradictory. I write in English
As you desired, and I suppose that you
Are as well acquainted with that language
As ever you were. Though I am not there
To speak it to you, I think we must agree
That many an ill encounter has been avoided.
When I call up thoughts of Ravenna—the Count,
Myself and you, as we made our few improvements
On marriage—can there ever have been found
Cavaliere servente as ill-suited
To the role? Here are arrived—English—
Germans—Greeks—bond and free—all kinds
And conditions in short, and all with something
To say to me—so that every day I have
To receive them here or go to find them
In Argostoli. Of the Greeks I can't say much

Hitherto as I should prefer not to speak
Ill of them—however much they do so
Of one another. I suppose despisers
Of Turkish despots will serve as well here
As lovers of Greeks. Messrs. Trelawny
And Browne are in the Morea—where they
Have been well received. Do not imagine
A soldier's grave for me—nor even that
An earthquake in league with the barbarian
Will send me and the Suliotes down
A newly opened path to meet King Minos.
I still hope to see you in Spring—meantime
Entreat you to quiet your apprehensions
And believe me ever your

   Amico ed amante in eterno + + + +

          N B

P.S. Pietro fell sick, but thanks to the attentions
of Doctor Bruno (whom we have rebaptized *Brunetto
Latini*, as he is rather pedantic), he is now
returned to a state of good health.

The Column

The first had been toppled she who
favored the austere style no curls
or Corinthian panache the caryatid
bearing an Atlas on her level head

understanding a world
She is the world also
the tree of the world
its bole and branches

the mother of mothers
Yet how few took note
when a gloved fullness
grew manifest a slight
entasis or pregnancy of

marble appeared beneath
the limewhite pleats so
that the massive sandals
creaked under its weight
accruing the living kilos
a bubble rising upward to

consciousness the dreamed
parenthood become virtual
(Each renounced conception
Michelangelo pared away to
free the soul held hostage
to stone only made final a
prison of flesh in marble)

With birth an unanticipated
blood is spilled but unseen
beneath asbestos robes hard
labor of that ploughman the
human mud turned up earth's
bleeding furrows from which
a new column springs lifting
its tassels into golden life

The harvesters come to bear away the grain
striding through fluted fields all unaware
of that invisible figure towering overhead
Her emblem is fashioned from the imagination and
built among high accumulations of autumnal cloud
I am the Goddess Ceres the Mother as Column am I

After Ireland: Five Poems

DUBLIN, THE LIBERTIES

Summer, and low clouds hang over the Liberties,
over chimneypots and glistening slates
an echoing carillon of competing changes
rebounds against into attentive skies.

What part of the trouble that Guinness made
was channeled into Lord Iveagh's brick
developments, old benefactions lived in
but ignored or forgotten? Prehistoric
the sniff of burning turf,
an earnest against the drizzle's
brief, underemphatic
scrim that steams over broken walls
where snapdragons volunteer
a red or mustard salvo—
on occasion, the tender valerian,
as mauve as the Sacred Heart.

In shops along The Coombe
faceted crystal and silver candlesticks
wait for those who can find pleasure
in things still useful, things antique;
and houses, for their owners
off at work or gone for supplies—
the dog within dozing on his paws
near scattered envelopes
beneath the letter-drop.

Slender stair rail!
hold up your newel, a small white globe
poised to catch from landing windows
one pearled highlight, and another one:

This sphere makes no forecasts,
offers no hints for future tactics,
but draws into itself each muffled, metronomic
step heard passing on the pavement,
much as to take the pulse of time,
but time not quantified, the one-way push of fact.

Rainclouds shake down tribute
for the Liffey, goods of water
to be trundled gray-green past Wood
and Ormond Quay, the traffic
in opposite direction turning
up Bridge Street right into High,
into the Liberties and the late afternoon.
Driving will be an effortless flick
of horsemanship, deferring almost never
to pedestrians, paired or single, who
make for home (each green or blue door affixed
with a knocker clenched in the bronze
muzzle of a bearded lion).

Dublin 8's promissory brick
is what they know, they have declared for it.
The knocker growls or rattles

as the master of a six-room castle
(not counting cellar and attic)
opens his door to greetings from the dog
and bends down through a backache
to gather bills and letters, hearing the old
wind-up clock plucking its wide-spaced ticks—
plural but otherwise out of number—
from the shadows at the foot of the stairs.

"NINA" AT THE PHOENIX PARK ZOO

Someone to watch? Pearl-cool, a tall carafe
Half-filled with ice and mist, she strolls, she stares:
At air-conditioned dens for polar bears;
At a vest-pocket veldt with shy giraffe.
White blouse, flaxen braids, *The Plays of Chekhov*.
Not the head you'd think would care for zoos.
But now she's asked a guide about the gnus,
The wolves, the bats; as if she meant to check off—
Hoof, paw, wing—each species of the Mammal.
"No platypus or lemurs? Nothing . . . bizarre?
"Well, then," she sighs and settles for a camel.
If she hasn't looked my way, that's by design?
(I'm standing near an ape named Zanzibar.
The cage that counts is his. And hers. And mine.)

TOWARD SKELLIG MICHAEL

In this half-embrace of earth, this
    pelvic amphitheater
of the Mother, St. Bollin's Well
sends down a brooklet whose chiming
    splash repeats morning office
    to the mist, a slow cowbell
tolling response from time to time—

    wholly spontaneous, like
the gentle collapse of beehive
    huts, their rounded drystone walls
    coaxed by the rough centuries
into simple forgetfulness
of form, a gannet's broken shell
    let fall as the tenant leaves.

Out toward Skellig Michael, the sea
    rises, the foregathering
clouds loose their blue-fringed shawls of rain;
like those that drenched St. Brendan when
    his landfalls along the Ring
    taught one fledgling mariner
how to step his mast and make sail

    for blessed shores to the west. . . .
Here, among stonecrops and smashed cells,
    each tomb's furnished with a door;

over which, the silhouette
of an ascending seabird or—
a crossbow, is it?—the fine dart
    tensed at musical alert,

    waiting to speed forth from exile.

STEPHEN DEDALUS: SELF-PORTRAIT AS A YOUNG MAN

No. I will describe the arts of flying:
   First the surge, an indrawn sigh,
Familiar windiness of all
   The sunlit death-defying.

   Peak, now sink to hover—
Roads and plots; rivers, beds where they crawl;
   The stink of altitude zero
Propels me up past clouds for cover!

Father of Icarus, claim your right
   To carpenter and be no hero.
But some have shed lost wax sincerely, and I
   Chose the son, who chose flight.

THE CHI-RHO PAGE FROM THE BOOK OF KELLS

CHRESTOS, or auspicious
To the Greeks, a pun for the Anointed,
Himself a Word with three aspects—

Or say an incalculable number of them,
Like the stars of the sky or sands of the sea.
Whoever's labyrinthine hand chromatically

Raveled this Chi-Rho for the Great Book
Of the Town of Kells (in Irish, *Cells,*
Or a monastery), let him expound how

A saltire may be drawn until flexible *X*
Takes the avatar of *P*, and conversely.
"In this Sign will you conquer," the motto

Floating underneath told Constantine—
Who set about, by whatever means, converting
Rome into that New Jerusalem, "The Golden"

By then a Roman casualty. . . . How intricate
The threads of history, tendrils of a living
Vine, web in knotted cords supporting the trellis

Of the words of life, whose letters may bear,
As on this parchment, a human face, the swanlike
Extensible throat spiraling into its letter

Like the crozier of a fern sprung up here among
Ranks of oriels, disks inscribed with prismatic
Abstraction, triskelia the funnels of visible

Melisma catapulting their spark and inwit
Across synaptic reaches through the plangent
Grace of ornament, which defeats constraint and limit

As it defines them, a skill made strong by trust
In the interrelation of all things dead and living,
Chiasm aspersed with chrism, its final and first

Principle scored in that polyphony, vocalic
And consonantal, of the stars in their courses,
The yet-to-be-deciphered music of the moving firmament.

Navidad, St. Nicholas Ave.

An infant quirk of a pine
with aerosol frosting, spangles,
and bulbs that blink red-blue-gold.
Manolito, three days home, they've put

in his picket-fence crib,
paper diaper cinched tight,
eyes squinted in a mask
that looks Chinese or in pain.

Asleep. Trailing sighs and smiles
they tiptoe out to where the Magnavox
screen extolls some *producto*
whose logo's a crystal star.

She glances up at the window
brimming with sodium light.
And, *mira,* snow begins to fall
like manna in the warming air

as from down the avenue a taxi
beeps a brass triad. Then an offended
wail summons mother, father,
todo el mundo back to his side.

New Year

Another year, another return—
Each one has drawn closer to home.
A perennial naif, whose pleased
intake of breath is meant to welcome
back the urban crush, prefers

familiar brickfronts and squares
even to vistas down the proud
colonnades and quays of Paris,
mountains lost among high clouds,
or domes at dawn in the pastel east.

These westward windows, fifteenth floor,
make a triptych frame for sunset—
which shows the buildings as somehow more
thoughtful than they often get
described as being; while the sky,

with blue impartiality,
may be forecasting the first
snowfall. . . . To sense purpose in turning
to the desk again seems right,
the crossed-out sentences and lines

summoning words and pauses always
nearer those that will be felt
as having stood by from the start,
waiting to assume their place.
The heat clicks on. Somewhere a bell. . . .

All the objects here have twinned themselves
with stories. The room's a cradle, or an ark;
it says that half the point of our departure
is coming back—suggestion followed by one
who breaks off work to watch the setting sun.

Notes

These notes are not mandatory but are offered to readers for whom notes will save time—a group that would have counted me as well, before I happened on the information contributing to the poems.

"The Band": the title may recall Browning's "Childe Roland to the Dark Tower Came," as well as incidents in the life of the author who said, "To have had the paradisal vision is to be ushered into a suffering world."

"Naskeag": Naskeag Point is a small peninsula in Maine, off Penobscot Bay. I did not know, the summer when this was written, that the name, in Abenaki, meant "place at the end."

"Two Travelers on a Summer Evening": the Sung dynasty in China had two phases, Northern and Southern. The Southern period developed in Hangchou, where the Sung court lived during the first part of the thirteenth century, looking back to the time before exile when the capital was K'ai-Feng in the North. One of the poets of the Southern Sung is Lin-Chi (sometimes known as Lin-Chi-Chi), a line of whose is quoted at the conclusion.

"From the United Provinces": Spinoza and Vermeer were born roughly three weeks apart in 1632, but the philosopher outlived the painter by two years, dying in 1677. His life had been threatened more than once, notably during his residence in The Hague, and his health was impaired from having breathed glass dust in the exercise of his trade as a lens-grinder. Vermeer's *The Artist in His Studio* (also known as *The Allegory of Painting*) hangs in Kunsthistorisches Museum in Vienna.

"The Candlelight Burglary": the sentence in quotation marks is recalled from Emerson's essay "The Poet."

"Dogwood": according to legend, the dogwood was the tree from which the wood of the Cross was cut—at which the species felt shame to the point of choosing never afterward to grow large enough to be used again for that purpose.

"Trout and Mole": *Salmo gairdnerii* is the species name for rainbow trout.

"Wild Carrot": another name for Queen Anne's lace. King Charles I was beheaded in 1649. The Umbelliferae are a group of wild and cultivated herbs, including parsley, carrot, wild carrot, and dill, all bearing flowers and seeds in umbel form.

"Maple Canon": the Greek word νοῦς *(nous)* means "mind," in the universal sense.

"Prophet Bird": a piano work by Schumann ("Vogel als Prophet") from the *Waldszenen*, Opus 82.

"Letter to Teresa Guiccioli": Byron was in the habit of signing letters with the initials "N B" (Noel Byron) perhaps because of the apparent duplication of Bonaparte's. Pietro Gamba, brother of Teresa Countess Guiccioli, accompanied Byron to Greece to assist in the Greek struggle for independence. Brunetto Latini is a vivid personage in Dante's *Commedia*—a poet and teacher who numbered Dante among his disciples. Many of the sentences here are to be found in Byron's letters for the years 1823 and 1824.

"AFTER IRELAND"

"Dublin, the Liberties": the Liberties are an old sector of Dublin, once standing outside the now vanished city wall. Early in this century, Lord Iveagh, the head of the Guinness family and the brewing concern that is the source of its considerable holdings, inaugurated a philanthropy for his employees, large blocks of solidly built housing. These are still maintained and lived in today.

" 'Nina' at the Phoenix Park Zoo": there is a large zoo in Dublin's Phoenix Park. Nina is the young aspiring actress in Chekhov's *The Seagull*.

"Toward Skellig Michael": Skellig Michael is one of the three small Skellig islands a few miles off the coast of County Kerry. It sheltered a monastic community from the sixth century well into the Middle Ages. The ruins of another small monastic community stands on the mainland at Killabuonia, near a spring called St. Bollin's Well. Originally a pre-Christian religious site, it comprises a group of beehive dwellings, a ruined oratory, and several tombs and crosses.

"The Chi-Rho Page from the Book of Kells": the Book of Kells is one of the most famous examples of medieval manuscript illumination in the knotted Celtic style. One of its pages is an ornamented rendering of the Chi-Rho monogram, a very old Christian symbol. It is formed by superimposing the Greek letters "chi" (χ) and "rho" (ϱ), the first two letters of the word "Christos" (the Anointed, or the Messiah). Actually, the monogram was used before Christianity as an abbreviation for the word *chrestos* ("auspicious," or, more colloquially, "OK"). It was the Chi-Rho that Constantine is said to have seen before the battle of Milvian Bridge, hovering over the statement "Touto nika" ("Conquer by this"). Tradition says it led to Constantine's conversion and then the adoption of Christianity as the state religion for the Roman Empire, with Rome as the administrative center. The "saltire," or cross of St. Andrew, is the X-shaped form of the cross, which appears often in religious and national iconography, since St. Andrew is the patron of Scotland.

"*Navidad*, St. Nicholas Ave.": St. Nicholas Avenue runs through Harlem in New York City.